SOULFUL SNAPSHOTS

Captured Moments and Echoing Tales

OBSERVING THE UNOBSERVED

NIRUPAMA GUHA

With deep emotion, I dedicate this collection of short stories to the cherished memory of my father, Late M. Ramakrishnappa. His thoughtful gifts of regional language storybooks were more than just pages; they were stepping stones that enriched my language skills, ignited the flame of storytelling in my heart, and deepened my understanding of various emotions. In every story of this book, his memory and legacy continue to be an integral part of my literary journey.

I also wholeheartedly dedicate this book to my father-in-law, whom I affectionately refer to as 'father without law,' Sri Tamal Kumar Guha, and grand mother-in-law Smt.. Rekha Bose. From the moment I met them, they provided unwavering comfort, making me feel like an inseparable part of the family. During the early days of my marriage, our evening tea conversations brought us closer until my husband's call to pick him up from the nearest railway station. These conversations ranged from stories of my late mother-in-law, his work life, my husband's childhood memories and engaging discussions about my own upbringing in Bangalore. Each day, I had the privilege of discovering something new about my new family and their unique, culture-rich, and value-based lifestyle before my marriage.

This book is a tribute to the remarkable senior individuals who have etched their indelible presence in my life, guiding the very essence of my storytelling passion. It's also a heartfelt acknowledgment of my extended family members, whose unwavering enthusiasm often outshines my own, each time I embark on a new venture.

Contents

Foreword

I am extremely happy to introduce my daughter in law Nirupama Guha as an author of short stories on NAV RAS or the 9 states of Emotional Empowerment.

Nav means nine and Ras means Emotions. As per our Atharva Veda nine emotions are :-

1. Shringar (love)

2. Hasya (laughter)

3. Karuna (sorrow)

4. Rudra (anger)

5. Veer (Brave)

6. Bhay (fear)

7. Vibhatsa (disgust)

8. Adbhut (surprise)

9. Shanti (peace)

Humans exhibit these emotions according to the situation that makes our lives lively without which we shall be just like robots. Our emotions flow freely (positive or negative). We go through them at different points of time. We react impulsively to a particular situation in the flow of emotions.

Nirupama has covered all the nine emotions of Nav Ras in the form of short stories (real life/ fiction) in a very simple language. She has a latent talent (not known to me) in creative writing.

I am sure all the readers will enjoy and appreciate the content of this book.

I wish her the best of luck in this new adventure and soon will place herself in the esteemed position of the literary world.

-Tamal Kumar Guha.

24 Oct 2023

Foreword

We are really happy to be a part of this book, and it makes us very proud to see our mom, Mrs. Nirupama Guha, achieve her dream of becoming an author.

The book is written in a way that's easy to understand and the stories are relatable. She's done a great job detailing everything and the best part is you never know what's coming next.

We wish her all the best and hope you all enjoy reading this book as much as we did.

-Aarya Aakash Guha, Aarav Aakash Guha

Proud Twin Sons

24 October 2023

Foreword

Soulful Snapshots by Nirupama Guha is a book about feelings. There are nine different feelings and you can see, feel and hear them in the stories.

Each story is like a tasty pancake made of feelings. When you read them, you learn more about yourself and think deeply.

I really liked how Nirupama put together each story with all the little details. After reading the whole book, I wanted to ask her if this was her first book because her stories are so full of life and interesting.

This book really captures important moments in life. It makes you feel like you've satisfied your soul's need to understand and think deeply.

I liked how each story started differently, and I couldn't stop reading until I finished the whole book in one sitting.

I hope Nirupama has more great changes and growth in her life.

-Pavan Bhattad, Founder of Knowledge & Karma

Foreword

If writing brings your soul on the paper, Nirupama's *Soulful Snapshots* has embossed her emotions into it through these stories. A book with various windows of emotions, reading it felt like a train journey where each story was like moving from one compartment to another.

This journey of 9 stories depicting 9 different emotions is a treasured chest of personal experience, which Nirupama has unlocked with her inner wisdom on paper.

I was wonder-struck with each story, as the way she has weaved emotions into them, the whole book seemed like a garland of phenomenal experiences in life.

Be it the story of Charlie or Sirina, every story is like a river which cleanses your heart and mind. While Nirupama has painted a rainbow of emotions on paper, I wish her many such masterpiece moments in life where her words become the beacon of hope and thoughtfulness for many more inspiring souls.

From soulful to soul-enriching, I wish Nirupama many such feathers in her cap of wordsmith glory.

-Dr. Mehernosh J Randeria, NLP Master Trainer, W3Coach

Advance Praise

"The NAVARAS [nine numbers of emotional states] have been dealt in an articulate yet lucid manner by the author for which I congratulate her. The subject matter is complex but it has been explained in simple free flowing story telling style, which not only captures attention but creates interest for the reader. For better understanding of human emotions, these short stories are a must read for all sections of readers."

-Pamela Nandi, New Delhi

"This is remarkable for a first-time writer, who is able to draw the reader in with her prose in an immersive way, and make them feel as a part of the story. Let's hope to be rewarded with more such stories in the future."

-Abubaker Koya, MD, Geberit India

"Easy read; reader can experience the emotions; give new prospects of looking differently."

- Dinesh Bhalkikar, Chartered Accountant

"The book communicates to you through simple, relatable and daily life stories, which everyone can relate to. At the same time, it subtly intrigues you to think about the level of consciousness with which you conducted yourself in each of those simple moments in context of your life. It's a powerful combination of simple writing and deeper questioning in life. Hope the book reaches millions and helps everyone understand with these simple and yet profound thoughts. All the best to Nirupama."

 - **Rajesh Yabaji,** Co-founder & CEO BlackBuck

"Wonderfully narrated stories; I emphasize on the word "narrated" and not "written" because it does transport one in the midst of the situation and stirs up the relevant emotion!

Would highly recommend...Absolutely a must read."

-**Bharat Chaba**, WayCool

This book beautifully captures the essence of human bonds and the power of perspective. The gripping chapter where Aarya unintentionally locked himself in a room had my heart pounding, only to be met with a powerful lesson in the end. Every tiny tale is gripping, heartwarming and navigates us in a way that makes us realize that Life is nothing but the "meaning we give it".

I believe this book will bring joy to your life and prompt thoughtful contemplation, ultimately enriching its significance.

- **Amrut Jadhav**, Founder, Brain Infinite.

"Life is full of surprises and shocks. Both of these create in us most of emotions. Learning can come from unexpected sources. So every reaction to a news by a person reflects a juice of emotion, like the tears that come out together but never meet, being divided by the nose as wall, like pearls of laughter that are held by lips, like the emotion of courage shown by strong shoulders and emotions of love that expressed by eyes..." **-Vasudev Behere**, Uganda

"Nirupama skillfully crafts a narrative that blends a meaningful exploration of profound themes with an infectious curiosity. Her writing invites readers into a captivating journey, fostering introspection and leaving a lasting impression on the mind and heart."

- Rakesh Aradhya, Learning and Creativity Coach

Soulful Snapshots to me is just like navratna and that definitely makes Nirupama the Akbar.

These Navratnas are 9 different shades of emotions depicted through 9 different stories.

Reading each story was like a thunderstorm of one emotion and I could see a bright and beautiful rainbow of self-reflection after it.

Despite being the first-time writer, I have witnessed a level-headed writing in Niru's words. My wishes to her for many soulful sojourns ahead in writing.

-Heena J Shrivastava, Book Coach,

Founder - Writernaama

Acknowledgments

In the beautiful voyage of penning this book, I convey my profound gratitude to my beloved husband, **Anando Aakash Guha**, and our amazing children, **Aarya Aakash Guha** and **Aarav Aakash Guha.** Their understanding, dedication, and self-reliance have been my unwavering support. I'm thankful for their resilience and emotional balance throughout my writing journey. Aarya and Aarav's hands are on the book cover, symbolizing the love and care they brought to my literary journey. They were also the first to read and review my stories as I continued writing.

I have been fortunate to encounter and learn from truly exceptional individuals on my life's journey. As I embarked on my second career chapter after a maternity break, my path intersected with extraordinary individuals who left a profound impact on my life.

It all began when I embarked on my second career chapter after a maternity break; **Abubaker Koya**, a youthful senior who rode the waves of life as an avid cyclist, was my ex-boss, a great mentor, he was inclusive and fleet-footed. He recognized my potential, which instilled in me the belief that I could achieve more in life. His guidance was like a gentle tailwind on the uphill climb of my career, propelling me forward with each pedal stroke.

In the midst of the 2020 pandemic lockdown, I crossed paths with **Amrut Jadhav** from Mumbai. He not only coached and certified me in memory training but also served as the cornerstone for my personal growth. Amrut, along with his dedicated team, is a 'memory awareness lighthouse,' diligently guiding the way to enlightenment for the entire nation, including the often-overlooked *adivasis* (indigenous communities).

Following this transformative experience, I had the privilege of engaging with **Pavan Bhattad,** whose extraordinary thinking abilities consistently chart fresh ideas and innovative perspectives. Pavan is a giver, much like nurturing rain. His approach to community-oriented teaching and awareness-raising is like a gentle shower of benevolence. He adeptly maintains a delicate balance, ensuring he cherishes his family time and sets a wonderful example of a father, all the while nurturing and inspiring his little twin sons with the gift of innovative thinking.

Guided by **Dr. Mehernosh Randeria,** a skilled NLP coach, I harnessed a versatile toolkit that transformed my personal and professional life. NLP empowered me with effective communication, emotion mastery and goal achievement. Learning to "Train the Transformers" using NLP, amplified my ability to inspire and guide others. This transformative experience under an NLP master profoundly enriched my life.

In the collaborative efforts of Pavan and Mehernosh, a remarkable addition was made - the introduction of **Heena J Shrivastava.** More than just a close friend, Heena emerged as my dedicated book coach, and her impact was nothing short of transformative, just like a skilled sculptor shaping raw clay into a work of art. As I set sail on my writing journey, she skillfully transformed every blank page into a thrilling new adventure, much like a navigator charting unexplored waters. Initially, the first draft was a solitary tale spun in my own mind, but with Heena's guidance, meticulous editing and her unwavering support, it unveiled the latent artist within me, like a hidden gem unearthed by a patient archaeologist.

As Heena played a pivotal role in shaping my writing journey, the rich literary traditions and culture of Bengal, a place where I proudly serve as a daughter-in-law, have deeply impacted my ability to see the bright side even in difficult times. These experiences, along with the unwavering support and positive outlook of my parents-in-law, siblings-in-law, and relatives, have also brought about significant shifts in my perspective.

My friend, **Puja** served as the lighthouse that guided me to discover the author within and her unwavering support propelled my book to new horizons.

I extend my heartfelt gratitude dearest friends and well wishers who generously devoted their time to review my work and share invaluable insights. These remarkable individuals have been cherished companions in the story of my life, with each one playing a pivotal role in shaping both my personal and professional journey. I hold them in the highest regard and with the deepest respect.

Nirupama Guha

24 October 2023

Introduction

Dear Readers,

Welcome to "Soulful Snapshots," where we explore a wide range of human emotions. This is my first book, and it comprises nine unique stories, delving into the depths of the 'nine emotions' or 'navras' - love, laughter, sorrow, anger, courage, fear, disgust, wonder, and peace.

I started this journey because I truly believe these emotions matter to everyone. They're like threads that make up the human experience, connecting people from all walks of life. These emotions are personal to me, guiding my own life, giving inspiration, healing, and a strong connection to the world.

My mission is to nurture empathy and foster emotional intelligence among readers. Each story is a mirror reflecting the intricate landscapes of these emotions, offering a space for self-reflection and personal growth. I aim to spark a transformation within those who delve into these pages, granting a perspective shift that can change the way they view themselves and others.

As you explore "Soulful Snapshots," I invite you to join me in observing the unobserved within yourself. May this book serve as a testament to our shared human journey, inspiring a deeper connection with your emotions and the world around you. Each story offers a reflection on captured moments and echoing tales, accompanied by three thought-provoking questions at the end of each chapter. These questions encourage self-reflection and provide space for you to journal your thoughts, emotions, and writings.

The reflections you gain from each story are sure to intertwine with your life's narrative, creating an emotional resonance that leaves you forever transformed.

With anticipation and gratitude,

Nirupama Guha

Soulful Snapshots - Stay Connected

Scan to visit my social media

1. Ganga's Gift: A Journey of Love and Courage.

Love is the bridge that connects hearts, and in its embrace, we find the courage to savor every fleeting moment

– Nirupama Guha

In the beautiful 'City of Joy' Kolkata, where the Hooghly River gently wrapped around the iconic Howrah Bridge, a special love story began to unfold. The bridge, like their love, was a strong connection between two different worlds. The river's ever-flowing waters reflected the changing stages of their affection. The sound of conch shells added a touch of tradition to the city, blending perfectly with their evolving bonding. Their story was etched along the riverbank, a testament to enduring love in a city where old customs and modern life harmonized perfectly.

Aditya, a young photographer who passionately wanted to capture the essence of Kolkata, couldn't resist the allure of the Hooghly's riverbanks. He set up his camera there, trying to capture the beautiful interplay of light and shadow on the Howrah Bridge. In those moments, he thought he was capturing the true spirit of the city.

One misty morning, as the sun struggled to break through the clouds, Aditya noticed a woman standing on the bank of the river near Howarh bridge, her silhouette framed against the rising sun. She exuded a profound sense of sadness, as though she bore the burdens of the entire world. Her name was Ganga.

As Aditya snapped a photograph of Ganga, their eyes met for a moment, and in that instant, something shifted in the universe. It was as if the river, the bridge, and the sun conspired to bring them together.

Days turned into weeks, and Aditya found himself returning to the same spot, hoping to catch another glimpse of Ganga. Finally, one morning, as the sun painted the sky in shades of pink and orange, he saw her again. This time, he approached her.

"Beautiful sunrise, isn't it?" Aditya said, trying to strike up a conversation.

Ganga turned to him, her eyes filled with a mix of sadness and wonder. "Yes, it is. But it's also a reminder of the passage of time and the fleeting nature of beauty."

Aditya was intrigued by Ganga's profound perspective on life. They began to meet regularly at the Howrah Bridge, sharing their thoughts, dreams and fears. Ganga had a secret, one she had carried with her for years—the knowledge that she had a terminal illness.

Despite her condition, Ganga radiated a contagious zest for life. Her desire was to relish every moment to its utmost, and her enthusiasm inspired Aditya to do he same. Together, they embarked on gastronomic expeditions through Kolkata's bustling streets, relishing the tantalizing street food like Egg Rolls, *Kabiraji, Puchkas,* adorned with tangy tamarind chutney on Park Street and the adjacent Camac Street. Occasionally, they indulged in *Alu Kabli,* and *Jhal-muri* during their *tonga rides* [Horse-driven carriages] on Victoria Memorial Road, delighting in the unique flavors that painted the city's culinary landscape.

But as their love deepened, so did Ganga's illness. She knew that her time was running out, but she refused to let fear dictate her choices. Instead, she lived each day as if it were her last, and Aditya stood by her side, capturing their moments together with his camera.

As the sun descended beneath the horizon and painted the river in a beautiful golden hue, Aditya escorted Ganga to the Dakshineswar Temple, a sanctuary of tranquillity and spirituality. Here, the fragrance of incense lingered in the air, and the temple's steps softly touched by the gentle waters of the river created an atmosphere deep of divine serenity. This sacred place held significance, as it was closely linked to the mystics of 19th-century Bengal, Sri Ramakrishna, and Maa Sarada Devi.

Ganga felt a profound sense of peace as they stood before the temple's sanctum. She whispered a silent prayer, thanking the universe for the love she had found in Aditya's arms.

As time passed, Ganga's health deteriorated further, and one day, she fell into a deep slumber from which she would never awaken. Aditya held her hand, tears streaming down his face, as he said his final goodbye.

In the end, Ganga had found her eternal peace, surrounded by the beauty of the city she loved. Aditya was left with a heart filled with bittersweet memories and a newfound appreciation for the preciousness of life.

Dear readers, I invite you to reflect:

A. Have you ever met someone who profoundly impacted your perspective on life, just as Ganga did for Aditya? What lessons did you learn from that experience?

....
....
....
....

B. Ganga's love for life was unwavering, even in the face of illness. How do you define the essence of living life to the fullest, and what prevents many of us from doing so?

....
....
....
....

C. When faced with the inevitability of loss, how do you think people find the strength to embrace life's fleeting moments and make the most of their time?

....
....
....
....

2. Beyond Metrics: Finding Happiness

"Laughter is the brush that sweeps away the cobwebs of the heart"

-   Mort Walker

In the heart of a bustling corporate office towered by gray walls and fluorescent lights in the thriving city of Bangalore, there existed a monotony that had enveloped the lives of the employees. The tech-savvy metropolis was renowned for its software giants, and amid this sea of spreadsheets and deadlines, there was one individual who stood out like a beacon of joy and enthusiasm. His name was Charlie, an unassuming employee who found delight in every corner of the workplace, no matter how mundane.

Charlie had a unique reputation. Even when his work performance metrics seemed lower than the rest, he was the one who brought energy and enthusiasm to every situation. He was the human equivalent of a shot of espresso, and his infectious optimism knew no bounds.

At the office, Charlie could be found everywhere but his desk. His favorite spot was the lounge area, where he would engage in animated conversations with anyone who crossed his path. He'd challenge colleagues to impromptu ping pong matches, and even during lunch breaks, he'd turn the humble cafeteria into a comedy club, cracking jokes that had everyone in stitches.

One day, Charlie's coworker Shelly became curious. She wondered how he stayed enthusiastic even though his performance metrics wasn't very good. So, during one of their leisure-time table tennis play time at the office, she finally asked, 'Charlie, how do you manage to stay so upbeat all the time?

Charlie paused mid-play, flashing a grin that could brighten the darkest of days. "Well, Shelly," he began, "I've learned that happiness isn't a destination; it's a way of life. I find joy in the little things, like a good conversation, a friendly match, or a hearty laugh. Life's too short to be bogged down by numbers on a spreadsheet."

Shelly pondered his words as they continued their game, and she couldn't help but feel a shift in her perspective. She realized that she had been so focused on her own performance metrics and the pressures of the corporate world that she had forgotten to enjoy the journey itself.

Over the next few weeks, Shelly started spending more time with Charlie. She joined him for lunch, participated in Table tennis matches and chess during their leisure time, and even found herself cracking jokes during meetings. Slowly but surely, she began to rediscover the joy in everyday moments, just as Charlie had.

One rainy morning, as they sat in the office lounge, sipping coffee, Shelly asked, "Charlie, what's your secret? How do you find joy even in the most challenging situations?"

Charlie chuckled and replied, "It's all about perspective, Shelly. We can't always control the circumstances, but we can control how we react to them. If you look for the silver lining in every cloud, you'll find it, and it'll brighten your day."

Shelly nodded, realizing that she had been allowing external factors to dictate her mood and outlook on life. Charlie's philosophy of embracing each moment with enthusiasm had transformed her perspective.

Dear readers, I welcome you to ponder:

A. Have you ever met someone like Charlie in your life? Someone whose unwavering positivity and love for life changed how you saw your own circumstances.

....
....
....
....

B. What valuable insights have you gained from these inspiring individuals on discovering happiness and humor in everyday situations? How have their perspectives influenced your own?

....
....
....
....

C. What Shelly would you need to take to become a source of positivity in someone's life, similar to how Charlie impacted Shelly? Please share your strategies and personal experiences.

....

....

....

....

3. The Power of Small Acts: A Kitchen Tale

"In a world where you can be anything, be kind."

-   Jennifer Dukes Lee

On a bustling Saturday afternoon, I found myself caught in the whirlwind of household chores. The clock struck 11:30 AM, and the realization hit me like a speeding train – I had procrastinated, and it was time to rustle up a hearty lunch. My husband was returning from a week-long official journey in the City of Dreams, Mumbai, and he was bringing along a senior officer we had invited for lunch. The menu was set, but it needed meticulous planning and execution.

I'm the kind of person who finds it challenging to decline when someone seeks help, especially if I can make a difference. Just as I was about to start cooking, my friend's call came in, right when we'd been talking about his career change for a while. This Saturday held significant importance for him.

Friend: (Over the phone, Anxious) "Hey, I really need your advice on this. It's a make-or-break moment for me today."

Me: (Politely) "I understand, but I'm a bit occupied right now. Can I get back to you later this afternoon?"

Friend: (Relieved) "Sure, I appreciate that. Take your time, however, I will leave a few text messages. Please check and respond; it's a bit urgent."

Me: (Assuring) "Sure, I can do that."

My phone rang, and it was a video call from my husband.

Husband: "Security check-in is done. We are seated near the boarding gate, taking off in another 30 minutes."

Before I could check if the menu was okay with him, he slid the phone toward the senior officer who was our guest for the day. We exchanged greetings and pleasantries, and I concluded by saying, "Looking forward to meeting you, Sir," with a broad smile. I then dropped a message to my husband, requesting him to please call me as soon as he lands or while taxiing so that I can start arranging the food on the table.

As I began gathering cooking ingredients, I realized I was out of Paneer & Ghee, a key component of two of the dishes. Typically, I would delegate such tasks to my husband when he did our weekly grocery shopping, but he was away. I had no choice but to order online, something I wasn't fond of. Amidst juggling between cooking tasks and responding to my friend's urgent messages, I quickly placed an order online. The clock was ticking, and I was racing against time.

Me: (Frustrated) "I hope this delivery comes on time. I really need these key ingredients in a flash."

I soon realized that I hadn't set a reminder for the delivery time since online grocery shopping wasn't something I usually did. Panicking, I checked the order status on my laptop. To my dismay, it said the order had been delivered at 12:30 PM. I rushed to the door, but there were no bags in sight. I felt a tightening in my throat, anxiety creeping in, my fingers went numb.

Me: (Anxious) "What do I do now? Should I call customer care? Should I ask my husband to follow up on this when he lands?"

My pre-teen kids had never handled an online inquiry like this before, and I was hesitant about asking them to call customer care. If I made them call, I'd have to guide them through the process of choosing options on the IVR and providing the necessary information.

Just as my frustration reached its peak, I received a call from an unknown number. It was the delivery person.

Delivery Person: (Polite) "Madam, I have arrived at your location."

Me: Rushed to the doorstep, I looked down towards the road and found him on a bike with a helmet on and a bag in his hand. "Why did you mark the order as delivered before you even got here?. Ok please come now and handover the items."

Delivery Person: (Calm) As he reached my doorstep at the first floor, "I'm sorry, madam. There was a railway gate closure that delayed me, so I closed the order to avoid further issues on my delivery timelines. But I have all your items."

As he took off his helmet, I looked at his face, I noticed he was bit senior in age, the few grey hair, and the wrinkles.

Me: (Guilty) "I'm sorry for being harsh earlier. Thank you for bringing the groceries."

Back in the kitchen, I couldn't shake off the guilt I felt for my initial reaction.

Me: (Reflecting) "I need to remember to treat people with kindness and respect, regardless of their age and profession."

This incident prompted me to gather my kids and share the story with them.

Me: (Thoughtful) "What do you think we should do in such situations, kids?"

Before my kids could answer, my friend called again.

Friend: (Urgent) "I really need your help. Can you please give me some guidance?"

Me: (Compassionate) "I promise I'll get back to you within the next couple of hours. Hang in there."

And getting back to my kids, I was reassured that Kids often have a unique perspective, and I was eager to hear theirs. They responded with empathy and understanding.

With a newfound sense of compassion and understanding, I returned to the kitchen to complete my cooking.

Me: (Reassuring) "We should always try to be kind and considerate, no matter what."

As I resumed my chores, my phone rang again. It was my husband calling.

Me: (Answering with concern) "Have you arrived?"

Husband: "Not yet, the flight is delayed by 45 minutes. Just wanted to keep you informed."

To my surprise, I felt a rush of happiness at the news of his delayed flight. It was a blessing in disguise.

Me (to myself): "That's great! I have some extra time now to get everything ready and to reflect on how love and compassion can make a big difference in our interactions with others."

After closing the pressure cooker, I took a moment to relax on my recliner. I also picked up my phone to respond to my friend's unread messages.

Our guest arrived with a gracious and welcoming demeanor, generously dedicating his precious time to imparting his extensive wisdom and providing invaluable educational guidance to my twin children. They engaged in lively discussions, spanning topics such as football, competitive exams, the significance of discipline, and early preparation for higher education.

Sir, also graciously offered glimpses into his early life, recounting his educational journey. He commenced his schooling in a regional medium before making the transition to an English medium for his higher studies. His passion for learning was vividly evident as he shared his profound love for books and an unquenchable thirst for knowledge, which eventually blossomed into an enduring passion for reading. His vast reservoir of wisdom and knowledge genuinely makes him a boundless source of inspiration and profound insight.

Incredibly, his passion for reading endures. He voraciously consumes various types of literature, including professional works and fiction. What's truly remarkable is his ability to devour novels in a single day, all contingent on the topic that captures his curiosity.

Despite having met Sir three years ago when he graciously hosted us in Mangalore, a sense of anticipation tingled through me, stirred by my husband's vague mention of the menu. I couldn't help but feel a flutter of nerves, as I wasn't entirely certain about his food preferences. My joy knew no bounds when I saw him genuinely savoring every dish I lovingly prepared and placed on his plate. As he departed in the evening, his warm blessings left us with a profound sense of gratitude and compassion.

Later that night, my friend called with exciting news –

he had successfully negotiated a deal with his employer. I could hear the joy in his voice, and it warmed my heart.

And there it was, the ripple effect of love and compassion that had started with a simple act of understanding, kindness and empathy had now extended to the field executives, our guest, the food we prepare daily, my friend, and my family. It made me realize that in a world where we often rush through our daily lives, a little empathy and patience can create a ripple effect of positivity, touching the lives of everyone we meet.

So, dear readers I invite you to reflect:

A. Can a single act of kindness or compassion, in a world where sorrow and sadness often prevail, create a ripple effect of positivity in our interactions with others, ultimately influencing the world around us?

....
....

....

....

B. How can we develop and nurture empathy and patience in our daily lives, especially during moments of frustration and sadness, to foster a more compassionate and understanding society?

....

....

....

....

C. In what ways do unexpected blessings or delays, like the flight delay in the story, offer us opportunities for personal growth and self-reflection regarding our attitudes and actions toward others, turning moments of sorrow and sadness into catalysts for compassion and kindness?

....

....

....

....

4. Rising from the Shadows: Sanaya's Triumph

"Anger is never without a reason, but seldom a good one"

- Benjamin Franklin

In the bustling hallways of a vibrant school where the joyous laughter of children usually echoed, a dark shadow loomed. This is where our story begins, introducing Sanaya, a quiet girl who found solace in the world of books and her dreams. Little did she know, her life was on the verge of being poisoned by the venomous presence of a boy named Jason.

Jason wore a mask of kindness, but beneath it, a sinister side lay in wait. The moment his eyes met Sanaya's, something within him stirred. What followed was a calculated torment that unfolded in cruel whispers and sly gestures, a slow burn that fanned the flames of anger within Sanaya, making her really angry.

One day, during lunchtime in the noisy cafeteria, Jason and his friends cornered Sanaya. They made fun of her lunch, calling it "weird" and "gross." Jason wore a mask of kindness, but beneath it, a sinister side lay in wait. The moment his eyes met Sanaya's, something within him stirred. The cafeteria echoed with their cruel laughter. Sanaya's anger smoldered like a dormant volcano, but she kept her words within, like a tightly sealed pressure cooker. This was yet another painful episode of her enduring their torment.

On a sunny day, while Sanaya was walking in the hallway, Jason and his friends blocked her way. They made fun of her, saying very unkind things, and their words were filled with cruelty as they laughed loudly in the corridor. This made Sanaya very angry, and she asked Jason, "Why are you treating me so badly? What did I do to deserve this?"

A heavy silence hung in the air, everyone waiting. Jason, who seemed to be in control of everything, was momentarily taken aback by Sanaya's audacity.

But then, his expression turned into a wicked grin. "I do it because it's fun, Sanaya. I like seeing you upset, that's my amusement."

Sanaya's anger roared like a wildfire, her determination crystallizing in that very moment. She would no longer be the victim of Jason's sadistic games. With newfound resolve, she declared, "It might be fun for you, but it's a nightmare for me, and I refuse to be your pawn".

The atmosphere grew tense, as if something big was about to happen. Jason and his pals, for a moment, were surprised by Sanaya's transformation and backed off quietly.

In the days that followed, Sanaya's anger morphed into her armor, transforming her into a resilient force. She refused to be a victim, and with her unwavering spirit, she doused the flames of bullying. The haunting echoes of torment slowly dimmed.

When Jason tried to tease her again, Sanaya stood up to him, and her words echoed through the hallway like battle cry. " You're wasting your time and energy, Jason. I won't let your bullying affect me."

As time passed, the bullying slowly faded away, and the darkness that had clouded Sanaya's life began to lift. She had transcended from a victim to a victor, proving that in the face of cruelty, one's resilience and determination could emerge victorious.

Dear Readers, I invite you to introspect:

A. How does Sanaya's journey from victim to victor inspire you to face challenges in your life with determination and resilience?

....

....

....

....

B. Have you ever witnessed or experienced bullying, and what strategies can individuals and society employ to combat it effectively?

....

....

....

....

C. Reflect on a time when kindness and compassion played a role in transforming a negative situation. How can we all contribute to creating a more empathetic and supportive world?

....

....

....

....

5. Courage in Kodagu: Sirina's Story

"Courage keeps the hope alive"

– Anando Aakash Guha

Nestled within the scenic Western Ghats of Karnataka lies Kodagu, also known as Coorg, affectionately referred to as the 'Scotland of India.' This captivating region has earned global recognition for its exquisite coffee and its valiant warriors.

Talakaveri, a revered site in Kodagu, holds the distinction of being the birthplace of the sacred river Kaveri, a place of immense cultural and spiritual significance. Coorg's rich and fertile lands are adorned with extensive spice plantations that yield a diverse array of aromatic spices. These fragrant treasures have been cultivated here for centuries, long before the advent of coffee.

Coorg's pepper has earned international acclaim. Kodagu's natural beauty and diverse attractions draw visitors from across the globe."

The region's lush forests, mesmerizing waterfalls, and abundant wildlife make it a haven for nature enthusiasts. Here, both Indian and international travellers come to experience the tranquillity and splendour of this remarkable land.

Our story unfolds in this enchanting land, where a spirited foreign adventurer named Sirina embarked on a journey that would test her courage and resilience.

During her journey, Sirina forged a bond with a loyal companion, Max, a faithful dog she had adopted during her travels.

However, Kodagu's serene beauty was soon overshadowed by the gathering storm clouds that heralded a relentless downpour. The heavens wept, sending down sheets of rain that showed no mercy. The tranquil rivers of Kodagu transformed into torrents, washing away bridges and roads, and turning the region into an island amidst an unforgiving flood.

During the chaos, Sirina's courage became her guiding light. While she had encountered nature's fury before, she had never seen this way. She watched in awe as houses crumbled, trees were uprooted, and the tranquil landscape was transformed into a battleground of the elements. In her heart, there was but one thought: the safety of her homestay, affected people at Kodagu, remembering her family member back in her home country. She could not connect with her families as telephone and internet connections were disrupted.

For days on end, Sirina found herself marooned in her homestay. While the rising water levels were rising up day by day , one day she heard a cry of a dog through her window. She opened her window and could not spot anything as the sight was covered with broken tree branches affected due to storm.

As she was stepping out of her homestay premises to check for the dog the staff members alerted her the dangerous conditions outside, nothing could stop sirina and she went out running on slides of mud without an umbrella. Sirina's courage was tested. She found herself walking towards the mudslides with a promise that she would find that dog and find out how she can help.

homes and rescue fellow residents, Sirina's keen ears picked up a sound that others seemed to have missed.

She spotted a dog balanced precariously on a makeshift rack in the floodwaters. With determination, she gathered available support and reached out to the dog, who looked at her with hope.

The piece of land where Sirina and the dog were stranded started loosening due to the force of the water. In this dire situation, Sirina's resolve remained unshaken. She screamed for help and even removed her red sweater, waving it in the air to signal for assistance.

Some people gathered and threw a rope towards her to rescue Sirina from the danger spot. With the support of a strong rope, Sirina made her way to safer ground, bringing Lucky, the dog, along with her.

Inside the room, she comforted Lucky, offering food and cleaning him up. The dog quickly adjusted to his new surroundings and grew comfortable with Sirina, even playing with her while wagging his tail. Sirina decided to name him 'Lucky.'"

As the rains finally subsided, they left behind a transformed landscape, forever altered by the force of nature. The devastation was profound, and Kodagu would require enough time to rebuild and recover. Through it all, Sirina and Max had survived, their bond stronger than ever. Together, they had forged lasting friendships with the locals, etching their story into the tapestry of Kodagu's history.

Sirina's adventure in Kodagu had indeed become unforgettable. she gazed upon the receded waters, Sirina couldn't help but feel grateful for every moment, even the most challenging ones. Threr was not a single moment that she had not thought about her family who lives back in her home country.

Dear readers, I urge you to think about;

A. When have you displayed courage and resilience in the face of adversity? What drove you to persevere?

....
....
....
....

B. Have you formed a deep connection with someone or an animal during challenging times that required courage? How did it impact you?

....
....
....
....

C. Recall moments where you witnessed kindness, resilience, and courage during difficult situations. How did those experiences shape your perception of human strength and compassion?

....

....

....

....

6. Unlocking Positivity: Aarya's Resilience

"The only thing we have to fear is fear itself."

- Franklin D. Roosevelt

In the quiet hum of my workplace, my colleague Bharat and I delved into the details of an upcoming investor visit. Time flowed steadily until the clock's hands aligned at 3 o'clock, a cue for my daily ritual. It was the time when I ensured the safety of my pre-teen kids as they returned home from school.

Typically, they'd send a message on our family WhatsApp group, but if it slipped their minds, I'd make a quick call to confirm they were safely home. During their final exams, I followed this routine, checking if they had lunch and how their exams went. They generally put me on speaker mode so that both sons could hear my voice. After a hearty meal, they settled down for the next day's revision and secured the main door, cocooning themselves in their shared world.

Being in the same class, these co-twin brothers often revised together, quizzing each other to gauge their progress. I reminded them they could take a short nap if needed before resuming their studies, and I hung up the call, trusting them to manage their time.

Back to my work, I was engaged in a discussion with Bharat. But after about 20 minutes, my younger son, Aarav, called me. As I answered the call, I couldn't help but wonder why they'd distract themselves during their study and nap time. Aarav's abrupt question jolted me, "Mum mum, did Aarya call you?" His tone was unusually loud and urgent, leaving me bewildered. Why would Aarya call me separately, and if he did, why wouldn't Aarav know about it?

My heart raced as I replied, "No, he didn't call me. *Ki holo?* What happened?" Aarav's next words caught in my throat, and my mind raced to comprehend their gravity. Aarya had locked himself in the bedroom and was unresponsive to the knocks and calls.

Panic surged within me, and I struggled to find my voice. My thoughts whirled with questions as I grappled with the shocking news. My kids had never locked their bedroom doors before. I urgently sought more details from Aarav. Had they fought or argued? What was the last conversation they had? How did Aarya seem when he returned from school? Was he upset or seemingly fine? Aarav reassured me about Aarya's exam performance and mentioned nothing unusual. I asked him to knock on the door again and call Aarya's name loudly. I stayed on the line, anxious and helpless.

Aarav's voice conveyed his frustration as he explained that he had already tried everything before contacting me. I immediately called the nearest shopkeeper Krishna, a familiar face in our neighborhood for over a decade. I briefed him on the situation and implored him to rush to my home and assist. I could hear Krishna, calling out Aarya's name, the desperation in his voice growing. I quickly called the carpenter and requested him to reach my home and break open the door. I was leaning on Aarav for more information, hoping to glean some insight on the situation.

Finally, I inquired which bedroom Aarya had locked himself in – the kids' room or our bedroom. When Aarav replied, "Parents' room," my anxiety deepened. We had never encouraged locking doors, and if they ever napped, it was usually in their own room. My limbs felt cold, and my heart raced. My mind raced, conjuring terrifying scenarios.

Krishna, sensing my panic, reassured me that Aarya was likely just deeply asleep. Still, I had an eerie feeling as I had to rush to my workplace's parking area. I struggled to control my emotions and inform my friend Soumya, who had been my lunch companion. Tears welled up as I shared the reason for my abrupt departure. My stomach churned, and my throat tightened, rendering me unable to speak further.

Soumya offered her support and decided to accompany me home. Meanwhile, Bharat, my colleague, had questions, but I could not muster the words to explain my situation. With great empathy, he understood the urgency of my child's predicament. Despite his busy schedule, he offered to drive me home. I said "no", appreciating his offer, telling him I would manage with Soumya's company.

Starting my bike, I called my husband, urging him to reach home as soon as possible, even though I didn't know what he could do. I received updates from Krishna that the carpenter had arrived and they were in the process of opening the door. As I rode towards home, my hands and feet felt numb, and I dreaded the upcoming call from Aarav.

His call came, and I answered with apprehension. His message was a lifeline – the door was open, and Aarya was in a deep sleep, undisturbed by the commotion. Relief washed over me. I called my husband to confirm the situation had calmed down, and he was on his way home.

Later that evening, I sat down with Aarya, my heart heavy with worry. I gently caressed his head and back, my voice quivering as I questioned him, "Aarya, why did you do this today? We were so worried, and it felt like we were trapped in the darkest of moments." In response, Aarya's voice carried a gentle wisdom that touched my heart. He asked, "Mum Mum, why did you focus on the shadows instead of the light?" His words left me in deep contemplation, wondering if it was possible to hold onto positivity even in the most dire emergencies, mixing relief with a newfound sense of wonder.

Dear readers, I invite you to reflect;

A. Have you ever found yourself caught in a moment of panic, and did you manage to shift your perspective from fear to positivity, as Aarya did in this story?

....
....
....
....

B. How do you handle unexpected challenges or emergencies, and what strategies do you use to maintain a positive outlook in such situations?

....
....
....
....

C. Aarya's response in this story encourages us to reconsider our default focus on negativity. What steps can we take to cultivate a more positive mindset in our daily lives, especially during times of crisis?

....
....
....
....

7. Deceptive Desires: The Price of Integrity

"Your reputation is what others think of you; your character is what you are."

- John Wooden

In the busy academic world, there was a lot of stress and rush in the air. The end of the semester was coming quickly, and every student was caught up in trying to finish their assignments on time. The work kept piling up, feeling like an enormous mountain to climb, and in the library, you could hear students typing away in a hurry.

In the midst of the hustle and bustle of assignments and projects phase, there was Akshi. People saw her as a dedicated student who always put in her best effort. However, her life was like a patchwork quilt, filled with family and part-time job responsibilities that made things more complex. Unfortunately, some of her insecure classmates used to tease her for missing a few sessions, even though they were aware of the personal challenges she faced. They even reached out to her family to confirm her absences from sessions. Akshi endured all of this but chose not to retaliate with negative people as these are unproductive activity while her family has been her great support.

As the deadline drew closer, her classmates rushed to finish their assignments, Akshi stayed focused on her approach. She put in a lot of time researching, working hard, and being creative on every project, always aiming for the best. While few looked for shortcuts and quick solutions through AI methods, Akshi worked diligently, sticking to her principles even with all the pressure around her.

One evening, in the library, Akshi overheard a conversation at the table next to hers. It was Bianca, a charming but manipulative student who knew how to get information from others for her own benefit. In a seemingly sweet but disingenuous tone, she was on the phone, scouting for valuable ideas, driven by personal gain.

"Hey, can you help me with this assignment?" Bianca said, her eyes quickly scanning the room to find someone who could give her valuable ideas.

Akshi noticed what Bianca was doing, and her discomfort grew. She had suspected for a while that Bianca was using her classmates to get ahead and seeking shortcut to success, but this was the proof she needed.

As time passed, Bianca kept using her classmates and making friends with those who had specific skills, taking their ideas without giving back. When Akshi, who valued fairness, asked Bianca about her assignments, Bianca avoided giving a straight answer, which wasn't unexpected.

As the deadline got closer, Akshi decided to see what Bianca was really like. She shared her unique ideas, stories, and themes for her project with Bianca, hoping for honest feedback. But to her shock, Bianca not only stole Akshi's ideas but also claimed them as her own, getting praised and recognized for her "creative genius."

Akshi felt a mix of disgust and revulsion as she watched her own hard work and creativity being presented as Bianca's, while she stayed silent. Her loyalty to quality and her principles were overshadowed by Bianca's dishonesty.

The days that followed were emotionally intense for Akshi. She felt betrayed by someone she considered a friend, and her trust had been shattered. However, this experience also prompted her to reflect deeply on competition, integrity, and the sacrifices required to uphold her principles.

Akshi was comforted by her mentors "I understand it was tough when your ideas were taken, but always remember, your unique execution and unwavering passion is what is going to set you apart".

Akshi felt better knowing that people who steal ideas usually aren't very creative and feel unsure about themselves. Their work is like a simple painting created by taking ideas from others, essentially taking what isn't theirs.

Dear readers, take a moment to reflect on your own encounters. Have you ever crossed paths with individuals like Bianca? People who manipulate relationships for personal gain, fail to acknowledge contributions, and engage in deceitful practices?

If you have faced such situations:

A. How did you handle it when you realized someone was using you for their gain?

....
....
....
....

B. Did you talk to the person about it or distance yourself from such people who lack moral and ethical values?

....
....
....
....

C. What lessons did you learn from intellectual thefts like Bianca?

....
....
....
....

8. Yana's Enigma: An Awe-Inspiring Journey

Travel is the only thing that makes you richer.

-   Unknown

Leading up to a long weekend, it was time to set on a road trip and utilize the quarterly budget set aside for team outings from the organization. I had a delightful surprise in mind for my colleagues. Each time we planned a trip, I made it a point to explore new and lesser-known destinations. On this occasion, our group consisted of 13 individuals, a mix of both seasoned employees and fresh faces, with men and women of varying ages. My love for exploring new destinations and the excitement of travel never faded.

I had meticulously organized an excursion to the Western Ghats of Karnataka, with a special highlight – a visit to the enchanting Yana. This destination had held a special place on my wish list ever since I watched the Kannada movie *'Nammoora Mandara Hoove.'* Yana is nestled in a remote location and gained fame following its feature in the film, particularly the unforgettable exclaimed line, "Manoj, This is Yana!" Those who were familiar with the area had wisely advised us to stock up on provisions 55 kilometers before our destination, at a place called

Sirsi. It was also recommended that we carry our water bottles.

As we set out on our journey, we were greeted by a tangible chill in the air. The road had become impassable for our vehicle, so we disembarked 4 kilometers away, marking the beginning of our trek towards Yana, leading us through a muddied trail, guiding us to the base of Yana's iconic rock formations.

In front of us, an awe-inspiring view unfolded: jagged cliffs carved from shiny black rock, creating a striking contrast with the rich, green Sahyadri Hills and the peaceful blue waters of the River Chandika. Our trail wound through a variety of trees and fruits, and we couldn't help but wonder which of these could be eaten. The journey was quiet; we hardly saw anyone else. The absence of shops, people and signboards heightened our sense of adventure.

The only guides on our path were faint footprints. We were surrounded by a jungle filled with different trees and fruits, and the birds sang a beautiful chorus of different songs.

While trekking, we came across a lengthy snakeskin, which initially startled some of us. The mere sight made me step back instinctively. However, with comforting words from my teammates, we quickly understood that there was no need to fear. The texture and patterns of the snakeskin told a story of a phase in the snake's life. This experience was like an outdoor classroom, teaching us about the marvels of nature and its enigmatic secrets.

We moved ahead. Along the way, we paused by a glistening water stream, its coolness rejuvenating our spirits before reaching Yana. The hike had been challenging, but our shared determination pushed tus forward. When they finally reached the caves, a sense of coolness and excitement washed over us.

Our astonishment grew as we marched towards the Yana caves. As I looked up to the glance of the pinnacle, a voice within me screamed "Nirupama, This is Yana!". A wondrous place in the Sahyadri hills of Karnataka's Western Ghats. These two gigantic rocks soared to a staggering height of 390 feet, and their jet-black color, due to karst limestone, held a unique charm. The lush forests and the serene Chandika River made the area around Yana a visual delight, perfect for those who love adventure and nature.

Inside the caves, we were greeted by enigmatic rock formations, leaving them in a state of wonder. Some believed these formations were the result of mythological creation, while others thought they might have formed due to volcanic eruptions. These diverse beliefs only added to the sense of amazement that engulfed the group.

Offered prayers at the temple here and we proceeded to explore the caves together, we created lasting memories, sharing stories, laughter, and even experimenting with calling our names loudly to feel the whispering echoes. We marveled at the wonders of nature, from the ancient rock formations to the hidden underground stream that seemed to sing its own melodious tune. Our journey was a testament to the power of teamwork and shared experiences.

As the sun began to set on our adventure, we found ourselves contemplating our journey. We couldn't help but wonder about the mysteries of Yana and the stories it held. These questions lingered in our minds:

A. What other hidden natural wonders lie in the vast landscapes of India, waiting to be discovered and explored?

....

....

....

....

B. How can we nurture a deeper connection with nature and appreciate its wonders in our busy lives?

....

....

....

....

C. In a world filled with diverse beliefs and interpretations, how does wonder and amazement bring people together, transcending differences?

....

....

....

....

As, we left Yana, the group was filled with a profound sense of nature's wonder. Our journey had been an adventure of astonishment and amazement, leaving us with cherished memories and a newfound appreciation for the beauty of nature. I was thankful for my mom and sister for choosing to watch this movie as a part of our family time.

I fondly recall one of the wise sayings from my NLP Coach, *"Movie nahin dekha toh kya seekha"* literally translates to "What have you learned if you haven't watched a movie?." It underscores the idea that movies can be a valuable source of learning and insight, offering viewers diverse perspectives and experiences that contribute to personal growth and understanding.

Dear readers, If you happen to visit Karnataka and nature lover, please plan a visit to Yana. The road extension has now reduced the trek to only 1.5km, happy exploring!

9. Sikkim: Land of Peace and Tranquility

Our journey through Sikkim reminds us that the highest levels of peace are often discovered in the unlikeliest of places, where beauty and calm reside

– from my travel diaries

The rhythmic clatter of wheels marked the beginning of our train journey at Sealdah Railway Station in Kolkata. We were excited for the Durga Puja Vacation and the Maternal family joining for this travel was an added joy. It was my first trip to North eastern part of India Sikkim, bordered by Bhutan, Tibet and Nepal is a state known for its Peace and Tranquility.

After hours on the train, we reached New Jalpaiguri and embarked on a thrilling four-hour jeep ride to Sikkim. The journey followed the picturesque Teesta River, with its calming blue waters and natural beauty. As we ascended into the mountains, the air grew cooler, and the scent of Himalayan pine trees filled our senses.

The road was challenging, but the rugged beauty of the Himalayas made it worthwhile. In Sikkim, we discovered colorful prayer flags fluttering in the wind, carrying prayers and a sense of peace.

We stayed in Gangtok, exploring the diverse districts of Sikkim, each with its unique charm. It is pa place, where every sunrise paints peace on the mountains. One night, we reached Lachen for a night's stay. We had to start as early as 4 am to reach the Gurudongmar lake and return before 12 noon, as the army prohibited tourists from staying beyond 12:30 pm.

The journey to Gurudongmar Lake was daunting, with high altitudes and challenging terrain. We arrived at the lake at 8:30 am, where the lack of oxygen presented a challenge. We had oxygen tests done at an army check point and were considered eligible to continue our journey ahead. The beauty of Gurudongmar Lake, situated at an altitude of 5,425 meters (17,800 feet), was breathtaking. A place where silence speaks louder than words.

Our 7 days in Sikkim visiting all four districts north, east west, sound were filled with exploration and adventure. We hiked through lush forests, visited ancient monasteries perched on hillsides, and marveled at the breathtaking views from high mountain passes. We had the privilege of being there during Navaratri and Durga Puja vacations, which allowed us to visit beautifully decorated Durga pandals.

As our week in Sikkim came to an end, we found ourselves reluctant to leave. The serene landscapes, the warm hospitality of the locals, and the deep sense of calm we had experienced had left an indelible mark on our souls.

Now, as we conclude our journey and return to the bustling cities we came from, we can't help but reflect on the importance of finding moments of peace and tranquility in our busy lives. In a world filled with chaos and noise, it's these moments that rejuvenate our spirits and remind us of the beauty of nature.

Dear readers, I would invite you to reflect:

A. Have you ever ventured on a journey that led you to discover the highest levels of peace and serenity?

....

....

....

....

B. Have you found moments of tranquility amidst the chaos of life?

....
....
....
....

C. How do you nurture the emotion of peace in your own life?

....
....
....
....

Epilogue

In our final story within 'Soulful Snapshots,' we witnessed Peace, just as we've explored all the other emotions in our journey. Like the unseen moments in our lives, these emotions are an essential part of the human experience. As we conclude our exploration of these emotions within 'Soulful Snapshots,' we are reminded that our feelings, our experiences, and our relationships form the rich fabric of our lives. Now, let's embark on a thought-provoking reflection about the profound significance of these emotions that tie us all together.

As we come to the end of this colorful journey that is life, we discover that our feelings are the threads, and our experiences are the hands that weave stories as unique and special as each one of us. These stories have provided us with a glimpse into the shared emotions that connect us all.

In the end, the nine emotions uncovered within the pages of 'Soulful Snapshots' are not mere stories on paper; they are the stories of our very existence. Our experiences, our encounters, and our relationships are painted with the vibrant hues of love, laughter, sorrow, anger, courage, fear, disgust, wonder, and peace. These emotions are the essence of our humanity, the rhythmic heartbeat of our existence.

Throughout this journey, I've learned that it's okay to be a person who expresses herself with depth and detail. I've learned that it's not only an innate skill but a unique trait that I've harnessed to create descriptive stories. Many thanks to Pavan Bhattad, to whom I once asked how to condense my words. His response highlighted the unique value in my elaborative communication style and encouraged me to identify the areas where it can be most beneficial. That day, I was already two stories old. The words of introspection encouraged further exploration in this literary journey. It's this inherent ability that, I hope, has successfully evoked the intended emotions within you in each of the story.

In sharing these tales, I also hope they've given you the opportunity to connect with your own emotional world, to ask profound questions, to seek genuine understanding, and to embrace the profound beauty of the human experience. For it is in understanding and celebrating these emotions that we truly connect with one another and, most importantly, with ourselves.

May 'Soulful Snapshots' inspire you to observe the unobserved, explore the unexplored, and celebrate the intricacies of the human heart. Thank you for joining me on this emotional journey.

www.ingramcontent.com/pod-product-compliance
Lightning Source LLC
Chambersburg PA
CBHW040106150726
48005CB00013B/1592